This JoJo & Gran Gran
storybook belongs to:

_____

First published in Great Britain in 2022 by Pat-a-Cake

Pat-a-Cake is a registered trademark of Hodder & Stoughton Limited

This book copyright © BBC 2022

JoJo & Gran Gran and the CBeebies logo are trademarks of the British Broadcasting Corporation and are used under licence

Based on original characters by Laura Henry-Allain MBE

Additional images © Shutterstock

ISBN 978 1 52638 391 4

1 3 5 7 9 10 8 6 4 2

Pat-a-Cake, an imprint of Hachette Children's Group,

Part of Hodder & Stoughton Limited

Carmelite House, 50 Victoria Embankment, London EC4Y 0DZ

An Hachette UK Company

EU address: 8 Castlecourt, Castleknock, Dublin 15, Ireland

www.hachette.co.uk · www.hachettechildrens.co.uk

Printed and bound in China

A CIP catalogue record for this book is available from the British Library

B B C

JoJo & GranGran

See the Moon!

pat
a
Cake

Picture Glossary

Here are some words from JoJo and Gran Gran's sleepover.

JoJo

Gran Gran

Panda

picture

crescent moon

half moon

full moon

tablet

bed

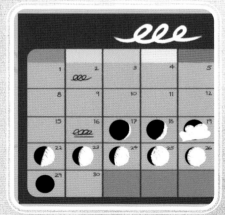

moon diary

It was an autumn day. The sun had set and JoJo and Gran Gran were having a sleepover.

"There we go, JoJo," said Gran Gran. "One big squishy bed."
"Thank you, Gran Gran. Please can I keep the curtains open tonight so I can see the moon?" asked JoJo.

"Ah, yes," said Gran Gran. "The moon is a very beautiful shape tonight."

"Gran Gran, the moon is a different shape to the one in your picture," said JoJo, pointing at the photo of Great Gran Gran on the beach.

Gran Gran explained, "The moon in the picture is a FULL moon, but the moon in the sky is a CRESCENT moon."

Gran Gran said good night and went downstairs. When she had gone, JoJo tried to go to sleep but she couldn't help but wonder where the full moon was.

"Maybe it's hiding," she said.
"Come on, Panda, let's find it!"

"The full moon might be hiding under the bed."

"No full moon here!"

"No full moon in the cupboard either, Panda," JoJo said.

It wasn't even in the chest of drawers!

"Where could the full moon be, Panda?" asked JoJo.

JoJo went downstairs to ask Gran Gran where the full moon
might be hiding.

"Oh, the full moon isn't hiding, JoJo," said Gran Gran. "Come on,
I'll show you."

JoJo and Gran Gran went back upstairs to JoJo's squishy bed.
Gran Gran brought her tablet, and showed
JoJo a picture of a full moon.

"The moon is a ball shape," said Gran Gran, "but we can only see what the sun lights up."

"Sometimes we can only see a little bit of the moon and sometimes we can see a lot of the moon."

"So when we see the moon in the sky, it can look like lots of different shapes," explained Gran Gran, "but it's still the same moon."

 said JoJo.

"All the shapes have different names," said Gran Gran.

"This is a crescent moon . . ."

"This is a half moon . . ."

"And this one is . . ?"

"A full moon!" said JoJo.

"You've got it!" said Gran Gran. "Now, good night JoJo - and try to keep your eyes closed this time."

At breakfast the next morning JoJo asked, "Gran Gran, will we see the full moon TONIGHT?"

"It will take more than one sleep before we see the next full moon, JoJo," said Gran Gran.

"Oh. How many sleeps will it be?" asked JoJo.

Gran Gran looked at the calendar stuck on the fridge, then said,

"I'm not sure. But, I think it's time

for a Gran Gran Plan."

"We can use my calendar to make a moon diary," said Gran Gran.

"Ooh!" squealed JoJo.

"Can you remember what shape the moon made yesterday?" asked Gran Gran. JoJo drew a cresent shape onto the calendar.

"That's right!" said Gran Gran.

"Now, this moon diary is for you to take home to Mummy and Daddy, JoJo. Later today, look in the sky and see if the moon is a different shape, then draw it here."

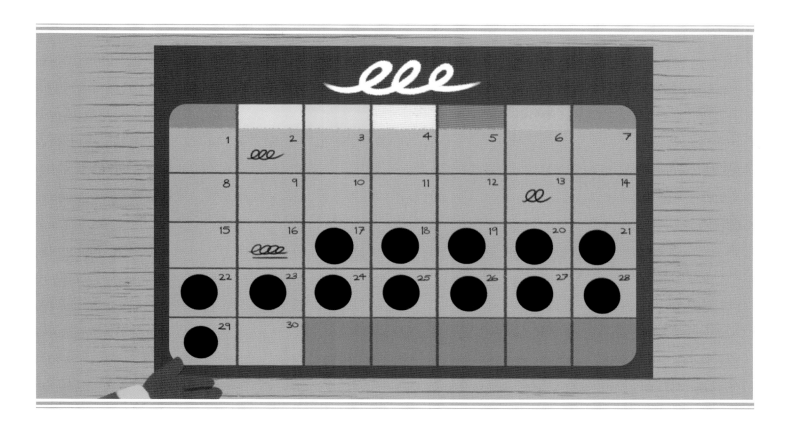

"And if you do that every day, soon you'll see the shape of the full moon!" said Gran Gran.

 said JoJo.

JoJo went home to Mummy and Daddy and EVERY night she looked
out for the moon and drew a picture on her moon diary, even
on the nights when it was too cloudy
to see the moon at all.

Then, it was time for another sleepover at Gran Gran's house. "I've brought the moon diary!" said JoJo. "The moon has looked like a LOT of different shapes."

"I wonder what shape it will be tonight," said Gran Gran.

JoJo looked out of the bedroom window and jumped up and down with excitement. "Look, Gran Gran! It's the full moon. It looks just like the one in your picture!"

JoJo coloured in the full moon in her moon diary.

"It was worth the wait, Panda!" she said.

In the morning Gran Gran said, "Did you sleep well, JoJo?"

"Yes," said JoJo. "And so did Panda."

"I'm glad we saw the full moon, Gran Gran!" said JoJo.

"So am I," said Gran Gran.

"And remember, whether you can see the CRESCENT moon, the HALF moon or the FULL moon —" said Gran Gran.

"— it's still the same moon!" said JoJo.

"I love you, Gran Gran," said JoJo.

"I love you too, JoJo," said Gran Gran.

Moon Diary

Monday	Tuesday	Wednesday	T
— ⚪	— ⚪	— ⚪	— ⚪
— ⚪	— ⚪	— ⚪	— ⚪
— ⚪	— ⚪	— ⚪	— ⚪
— ⚪	— ⚪	— ⚪	

Make your very own moon diary! Draw the shape of the moon that you see onto the circles below and colour in the dark sky. Can you see a full moon?

y	Friday	Saturday	Sunday
	— ⬤	— ⬤	— ⬤
	— ⬤	— ⬤	— ⬤
	— ⬤	— ⬤	— ⬤
	— ⬤	— ⬤	— ⬤